3/2007

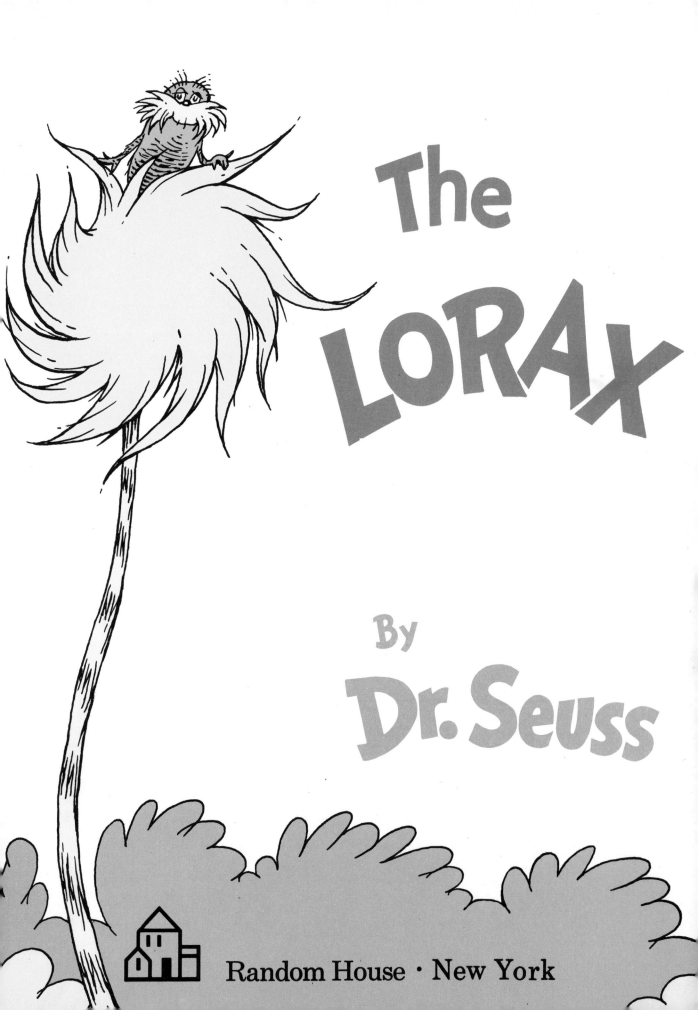

The
LORAX

By
Dr. Seuss

Random House · New York

For Audrey, Lark and Lea

With Love

Published in the United States by Random House, Inc., New York,
and simultaneously in Canada by Random House of Canada Limited, Toronto.

This title was originally cataloged by the Library of Congress as follows:
Geisel, Theodor Seuss, 1904– The Lorax, by Dr. Seuss. New York, Random House [1971] [70]
p. col. illus. 29 cm. SUMMARY: The Once-ler describes the results of the local pollution problem.
[1. Stories in rhyme] I. Title. PZ8.3.G276Lo [E] 74-158378
ISBN: 0-394-82337-0 (trade) ; 0-394-92337-5 (lib. bdg.)

Manufactured in the United States of America

64 65 66 67 68 69 70

At the far end of town
where the Grickle-grass grows
and the wind smells slow-and-sour when it blows
and no birds ever sing excepting old crows...
is the Street of the Lifted Lorax.

And deep in the Grickle-grass, some people say,
if you look deep enough you can still see, today,
where the Lorax once stood
just as long as it could
before somebody lifted the Lorax away.

What *was* the Lorax?
And why was it there?
And why was it lifted and taken somewhere
from the far end of town where the Grickle-grass grows?
The old Once-ler still lives here.
Ask him. *He* knows.

You won't see the Once-ler.
Don't knock at his door.
He stays in his Lerkim on top of his store.
He lurks in his Lerkim, cold under the roof,
where he makes his own clothes
out of miff-muffered moof.
And on special dank midnights in August,
he peeks
out of the shutters
and sometimes he speaks
and tells how the Lorax was lifted away.

He'll tell you, perhaps…
if you're willing to pay.

On the end of a rope
he lets down a tin pail
and you have to toss in fifteen cents
and a nail
and the shell of a great-great-great-
grandfather snail.

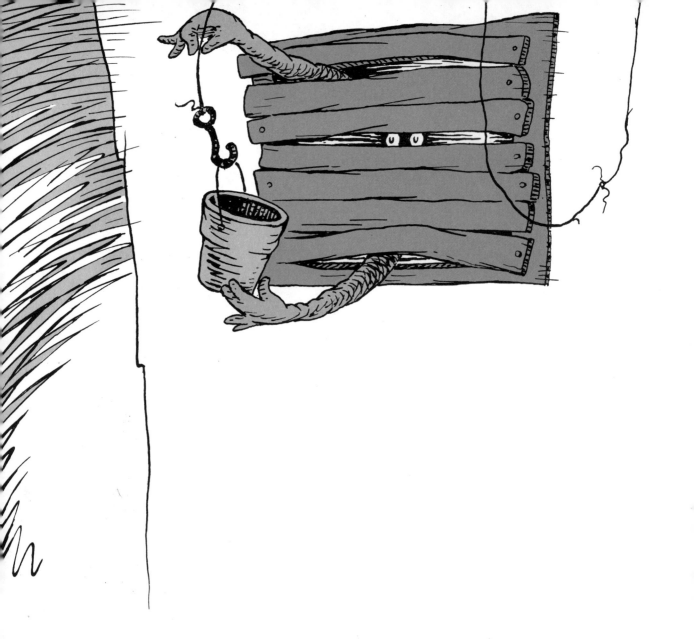

Then he pulls up the pail,
makes a most careful count
to see if you've paid him
the proper amount.

Then he hides what you paid him
away in his Snuvv,
his secret strange hole
in his gruvvulous glove.

Then he grunts, "I will call you by Whisper-ma-Phone,
for the secrets I tell are for your ears alone."

SLUPP!
Down slupps the Whisper-ma-Phone to your ear
and the old Once-ler's whispers are not very clear,
since they have to come down
through a snergelly hose,
and he sounds
as if he had
smallish bees up his nose.

"Now I'll tell you," he says, with his teeth sounding gray,
"how the Lorax got lifted and taken away...

    It all started way back...
    such a long, long time back...

Way back in the days when the grass was still green
and the pond was still wet
and the clouds were still clean,
and the song of the Swomee-Swans rang out in space…
one morning, I came to this glorious place.
And I first saw the trees!
The Truffula Trees!
The bright-colored tufts of the Truffula Trees!
Mile after mile in the fresh morning breeze.

ONCE-LER
WAGON

And, under the trees, I saw Brown Bar-ba-loots
frisking about in their Bar-ba-loot suits
as they played in the shade and ate Truffula Fruits.

From the rippulous pond
came the comfortable sound
of the Humming-Fish humming
while splashing around.

But those *trees!* Those *trees!*
Those Truffula Trees!
All my life I'd been searching
for trees such as these.
The touch of their tufts
was much softer than silk.
And they had the sweet smell
of fresh butterfly milk.

I felt a great leaping
of joy in my heart.
I knew just what I'd do!
I unloaded my cart.

In no time at all, I had built a small shop.
Then I chopped down a Truffula Tree with one chop.
And with great skillful skill and with great speedy speed,
I took the soft tuft. And I knitted a Thneed!

The instant I'd finished, I heard a *ga-Zump!*
I looked.
I saw something pop out of the stump
of the tree I'd chopped down. It was sort of a man.
Describe him?... That's hard. I don't know if I can.

He was shortish. And oldish.
And brownish. And mossy.
And he spoke with a voice
that was sharpish and bossy.

"Mister!" he said with a sawdusty sneeze,
"I am the Lorax. I speak for the trees.
I speak for the trees, for the trees have no tongues.
And I'm asking you, sir, at the top of my lungs"—
he was very upset as he shouted and puffed—
"*What's that THING you've made out of my Truffula tuft?*"

"Look, Lorax," I said. "There's no cause for alarm.
I chopped just one tree. I am doing no harm.
I'm being quite useful. This thing is a Thneed.
A Thneed's a Fine-Something-That-All-People-Need!
It's a shirt. It's a sock. It's a glove. It's a hat.
But it has *other* uses. Yes, far beyond that.
You can use it for carpets. For pillows! For sheets!
Or curtains! Or covers for bicycle seats!"

    The Lorax said,
    "Sir! You are crazy with greed.
    There is no one on earth
    who would buy that fool Thneed!"

But the very next minute I proved he was wrong.
For, just at that minute, a chap came along,
and he thought that the Thneed I had knitted was great.
He happily bought it for three ninety-eight.

I laughed at the Lorax, "You poor stupid guy!
You never can tell what some people will buy."

"I repeat," cried the Lorax,
"I speak for the trees!"

"I'm busy," I told him.
"Shut up, if you please."

I rushed 'cross the room, and in no time at all,
built a radio-phone. I put in a quick call.
I called all my brothers and uncles and aunts
and I said, "Listen here! Here's a wonderful chance
for the whole Once-ler Family to get mighty rich!
Get over here fast! Take the road to North Nitch.
Turn left at Weehawken. Sharp right at South Stitch."

And, in no time at all,
in the factory I built,
the whole Once-ler Family
was working full tilt.
We were all knitting Thneeds
just as busy as bees,
to the sound of the chopping
of Truffula Trees.

Then...
Oh! Baby! Oh!
How my business did grow!
Now, chopping one tree
at a time
was too slow.

So I quickly invented my Super-Axe-Hacker
which whacked off four Truffula Trees at one smacker.
We were making Thneeds
four times as fast as before!
And that Lorax?...
He didn't show up any more.

But the next week
he knocked
on my new office door.

He snapped, "I'm the Lorax who speaks for the trees
which you seem to be chopping as fast as you please.
But I'm *also* in charge of the Brown Bar-ba-loots
who played in the shade in their Bar-ba-loot suits
and happily lived, eating Truffula Fruits.

"NOW...thanks to your hacking my trees to the ground,
there's not enough Truffula Fruit to go 'round.
And my poor Bar-ba-loots are all getting the crummies
because they have gas, and no food, in their tummies!

"They loved living here. But I can't let them stay.
They'll have to find food. And I hope that they may.
Good luck, boys," he cried. And he sent them away.

I, the Once-ler, felt sad
as I watched them all go.
BUT...
business is business!
And business must grow
regardless of crummies in tummies, you know.

I meant no harm. I most truly did not.
But I had to grow bigger. So bigger I got.
I biggered my factory. I biggered my roads.
I biggered my wagons. I biggered the loads
of the Thneeds I shipped out. I was shipping them forth
to the South! To the East! To the West! To the North!
I went right on biggering...selling more Thneeds.
And I biggered my money, which everyone needs.

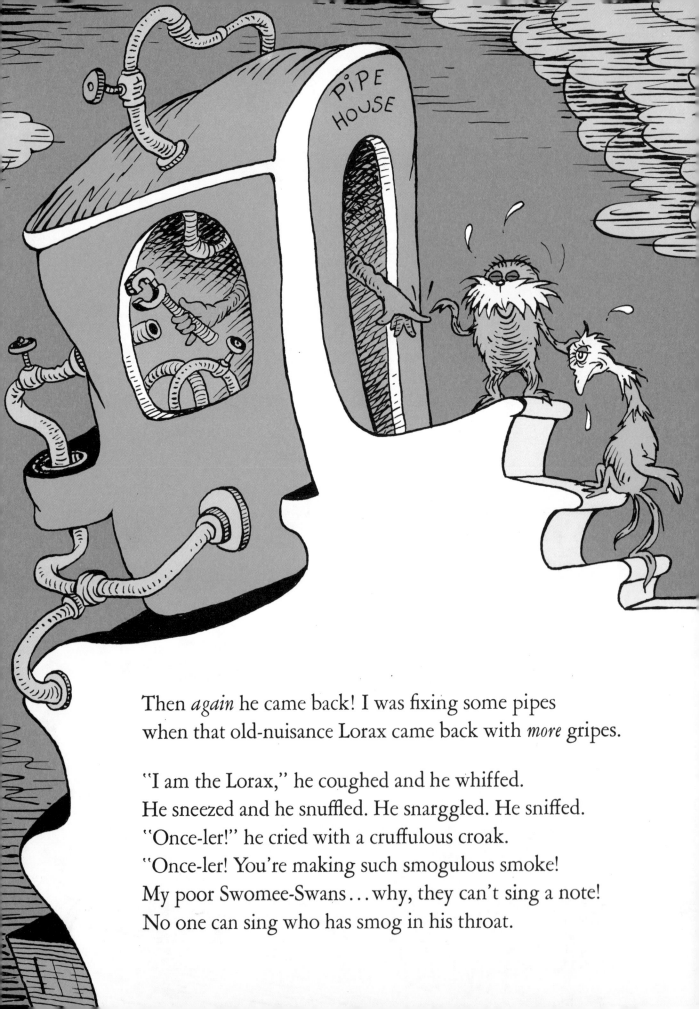

Then *again* he came back! I was fixing some pipes
when that old-nuisance Lorax came back with *more* gripes.

"I am the Lorax," he coughed and he whiffed.
He sneezed and he snuffled. He snarggled. He sniffed.
"Once-ler!" he cried with a cruffulous croak.
"Once-ler! You're making such smogulous smoke!
My poor Swomee-Swans...why, they can't sing a note!
No one can sing who has smog in his throat.

"And so," said the Lorax,
"—please pardon my cough—
they cannot live here.
So I'm sending them off.

"Where will they go?…
I don't hopefully know.

They may have to fly for a month…or a year…
To escape from the smog you've smogged-up around here.

"What's *more*," snapped the Lorax. (His dander was up.)
"Let me say a few words about Gluppity-Glupp.
Your machinery chugs on, day and night without stop
making Gluppity-Glupp. Also Schloppity-Schlopp.
And what do you do with this leftover goo?...
I'll show you. You dirty old Once-ler man, you!

"You're glumping the pond where the Humming-Fish hummed!
No more can they hum, for their gills are all gummed.
So I'm sending them off. Oh, their future is dreary.
They'll walk on their fins and get woefully weary
in search of some water that isn't so smeary."

And then I got mad.
I got terribly mad.
I yelled at the Lorax, "Now listen here, Dad!
All you do is yap-yap and say, 'Bad! Bad! Bad! Bad!'
Well, I have my rights, sir, and I'm telling *you*
I intend to go on doing just what I do!
And, for your information, you Lorax, I'm figgering
on biggering

    and BIGGERING

       and **BIGGERING**

          and **BIGGERING**,

turning MORE Truffula Trees into Thneeds
which everyone, EVERYONE, *EVERYONE* needs!"

And at that very moment, we heard a loud whack!
From outside in the fields came a sickening smack
of an axe on a tree. Then we heard the tree fall.
The very last Truffula Tree of them all!

No more trees. No more Thneeds. No more work to be done.
So, in no time, my uncles and aunts, every one,
all waved me good-bye. They jumped into my cars
and drove away under the smoke-smuggered stars.

Now all that was left 'neath the bad-smelling sky
was my big empty factory...
the Lorax...
and I.

The Lorax said nothing. Just gave me a glance…
just gave me a very sad, sad backward glance…
as he lifted himself by the seat of his pants.
And I'll never forget the grim look on his face
when he heisted himself and took leave of this place,
through a hole in the smog, without leaving a trace.

THNEEDS

THNEEDS

And all that the Lorax left here in this mess
was a small pile of rocks, with the one word...
"UNLESS."
Whatever *that* meant, well, I just couldn't guess.

That was long, long ago.
But each day since that day
I've sat here and worried
and worried away.
Through the years, while my buildings
have fallen apart,
I've worried about it
with all of my heart.

"But *now*," says the Once-ler,
"Now that *you're* here,
the word of the Lorax seems perfectly clear.
UNLESS someone like you
cares a whole awful lot,
nothing is going to get better.
It's not.

"SO...

Catch!" calls the Once-ler.
He lets something fall.
"It's a Truffula Seed.
It's the last one of all!
You're in charge of the last of the Truffula Seeds.
And Truffula Trees are what everyone needs.
Plant a new Truffula. Treat it with care.
Give it clean water. And feed it fresh air.
Grow a forest. Protect it from axes that hack.
Then the Lorax
and all of his friends
may come back."